Teddy Flies Away

by Molly Brett

Teddy Bear felt very sad. A new doll had arrived
for his owner's birthday and
she had been taken on a visit to Granny, while poor
Teddy was left behind.

He watched the car drive out of the gate
and wondered what he could do all day with
nobody to play with him.

Some of the toys began to spring clean the dolls' house.
Others had a ride on the rocking horse
but there was not room for Teddy.

"I'll go for a ride all by myself," he growled,
        getting out a toy motor car
            but – he was too fat to fit into it.

So he tried to drive the tractor but – once
started it would not stop and careered round
and round the floor.

"Stop! Stop!" squeaked the little bear. The other
toys hung on behind and then a wheel
came off while Teddy fell out with a big bump.

Then he saw a red balloon left behind after the birthday
party; there was not much air
in it so he started to blow it up.

He blew and he blew and the balloon got bigger and bigger.
Then it rose in the air and floated out of the
window with Teddy Bear
holding on tight to the string.

He flew over the garden,
waving his paw to the birds,

But he landed quite safely on a big waterlily leaf.
"Better ducks than a ducking!" chuckled Teddy
as they swam round him quacking with surprise.

Next moment he was jerked into the air again and
blown far away and then he saw the sea below.

A crowd of gulls flew round the balloon with loud
squawks; they thought here
was something nice to eat and started to peck it.

There was a loud POP! as the balloon
burst and down fell Teddy expecting
to plunge into the waves.

18

But no – he landed on the beach and what fun it was to be
there! Then he found a child's spade washed up
by the tide, and was soon digging a fine sand castle.

19

"Now I am King of the Castle and here I shall
stay," chuckled the little bear, sitting
on top of it.

But the sea soon washed it all away.

So Teddy found a small cave, "this will make a fine house,"
he thought and then water came
swishing in and he had to paddle out on a piece of drift wood.

His paws were wet and cold so he started to walk home.
But it was getting dark and the little bear
was tired, so he sat down in tears, while woodland
animals tried to comfort him.

Then a large owl flew over to see what was the matter.

"Cheer up," he hooted,
"and I'll soon take you home on my back."

23

The kind owl flew on silent wings high above the road, which
passed near Teddy's house, and left him
safely on the window sill.
He climbed in just before his owner came to take him to bed.
"Grannie liked my new doll," she said, "but she
wants to see *you* next time Teddy," and then they both went to sleep.